First published 2010 by Walker Books Ltd, 87 Vauxhall Walk, London SE11 5HJ

1 3 5 7 9 10 8 6 4 2

© 2010 Yoko Shima

The right of Yoko Shima to be identified as author/illustrator of this work has been asserted
by her in accordance with the Copyright, Designs and Patents Act 1988

This book has been typeset in Godlike
Printed in China

British Library Cataloguing in Publication Data:
a catalogue record for this book is available from the British Library

ISBN 978-1-4063-2326-9

www.walker.co.uk

DEDICATED TO MY DOG MEWCHAS

Sniff

YOKOCOCO

WALKER BOOKS

AND SUBSIDIARIES

LONDON · BOSTON · SYDNEY · AUCKLAND

"Fennel has got Granny's slipper
on his nose again!" said Vincent.

"Where are you going today, Fennel?" asked Mum.

"Sniff," said Fennel and set off.

Fennel came to the park.

He sat on a bench looking at the pond.

"Do you feel lonely too?" asked the old man.

"Sniff," said Fennel.

Fennel walked to the railway station.

A bird asked,

"Does the slipper smell nice?"

"Sniff," said Fennel.

Fennel got on the train.

He looked out of the window.

"Have you got a ticket?" asked the guard.

"Sniff," said Fennel.

The train reached
the end of the line.
"What's happened to your nose?"
asked a dog.
"Sniff," said Fennel.

Fennel walked to the beach.

"How can you smell the sea with a slipper

on your nose?" asked the girl.

"Sniff," said Fennel.

The sun was setting. It was so beautiful.

"Sniff," said Fennel,

and a tear rolled down his cheek.

Fennel sat there until it was dark.

It was quiet.

After a while he stood up and walked away.

Fennel got on the train.

"Did you enjoy your trip?" asked the guard.

"Sniff," said Fennel.

Fennel reached home at last.

"You are very late today," said Dad.

"We've been worried about you,"

said Vincent.

"Sniff," said Fennel.

Fennel put the slipper back down

in its place.

And he curled up beside Granny's chair

just like he always did

when Granny used to sit there.

"We all miss Granny
but we are here, Fennel,"
said Mum.

"And we love you too,"
said Vincent.

"Woof!" said Fennel.